P9-DNE-264

A TALE FROM
WINNIE-THE-POOH
AND A SMACKEREL OF VERSE

A. A. MILNE

A TALE FROM
WINNIE-THE-POOH
AND A SMACKEREL OF VERSE

With Decorations by Ernest H. Shepard

penguin books

PENGUIN BOOKS
Published by the Penguin Group
Penguin Books USA Inc., 375 Hudson Street,
New York, New York 10014, U.S.A
Penguin Books Ltd, 27 Wrights Lane,
London W8 5TZ, England
Penguin Books Australia Ltd, Ringwood,
Victoria, Australia
Penguin Books Canada Ltd, 10 Alcorn Avenue,
Toronto, Ontario, Canada M4V 3B2
Penguin Books (N.Z.) Ltd, 182–190 Wairau Road,
Auckland 10, New Zealand

Penguin Books Ltd, Registered Offices:
Harmondsworth, Middlesex, England

Published in Penguin Books 1995

Individual copyright for text and illustrations:
When We Were Very Young, copyright © 1924, by
E. P. Dutton & Co., Inc.;
copyright renewal 1952 by A. A. Milne.
Winnie-the-Pooh, copyright © 1926 by E. P. Dutton & Co., Inc.;
copyright renewal 1954 by A. A. Milne.
Now We Are Six, copyright © 1927 by E. P. Dutton & Co., Inc.;
copyright renewal 1955 by A. A. Milne.
All rights reserved

ISBN 0 14 60.0104 4

Printed in the United States of America

Except in the United States of America, this book is sold subject to the
condition that it shall not, by way of trade or otherwise, be lent, re-sold,
hired out, or otherwise circulated without the publisher's prior consent
in any form of binding or cover other than that in which it is published
and without a similar condition including this condition being imposed
on the subsequent purchaser.

The story appearing in this edition is taken from *Winnie-the-Pooh*, and the poems are from *When We Were Very Young* and *Now We Are Six*. Those titles, along with *The House At Pooh Corner*, are available in hardcover from Dutton Children's Books and in paperback from Puffin Books.

CONTENTS

A TALE FROM
WINNIE-THE-POOH
AND A SMACKEREL OF VERSE

IN WHICH *We Are Introduced to Winnie-the-Pooh and Some Bees, and the Stories Begin*

Here is Edward Bear, coming downstairs now, bump, bump, bump, on the back of his head, behind Christopher Robin. It is, as far as he knows, the only way of coming downstairs, but sometimes he feels that there really is another way, if only he could stop bumping for a moment and think of it. And then he feels that perhaps there isn't. Anyhow, here he is at the bottom, and ready to be introduced to you. Winnie-the-Pooh.

When I first heard his name, I said, just as you are going to say, "But I thought he was a boy?"

"So did I," said Christopher Robin.

"Then you can't call him Winnie?"

"I don't."

"But you said——"

"He's Winnie-ther-Pooh. Don't you know what *'ther'* means?"

"Ah, yes, now I do," I said quickly; and I hope you do too, because it is all the explanation you are going to get.

Sometimes Winnie-the-Pooh likes a game of some sort when he comes downstairs, and sometimes he likes to sit quietly in front of the fire and listen to a story. This evening——

"What about a story?" said Christopher Robin.

"What about a story?" I said.

"Could you very sweetly tell Winnie-the-Pooh one?"

"I suppose I could," I said. "What sort of stories does he like?"

"About himself. Because he's *that* sort of Bear."

"Oh, I see."

"So could you very sweetly?"

"I'll try," I said.

So I tried.

. . . . .

Once upon a time, a very long time ago now, about last Friday, Winnie-the-Pooh lived in a forest all by himself under the name of Sanders.

(*"What does 'under the name' mean?" asked Christopher Robin.*

"It means he had the name over the door in gold letters, and lived under it."

"Winnie-the-Pooh wasn't quite sure," said Christopher Robin.

"Now I am," said a growly voice.

"Then I will go on," said I.)

. . . . .

One day when he was out walking, he came to an open place in the middle of the forest, and in the middle of this place was a large oak-tree, and, from the top of the tree, there came a loud buzzing-noise.

Winnie-the-Pooh sat down at the foot of the tree, put his head between his paws and began to think.

First of all he said to himself: "That buzzing-noise means something. You don't get a buzzing-noise like that, just buzzing and buzzing, without its meaning something. If

there's a buzzing-noise, somebody's making a buzzing-noise, and the only reason for making a buzzing-noise that *I* know of is because you're a bee."

Then he thought another long time, and said: "And the only reason for being a bee that I know of is making honey."

And then he got up, and said, "And the only reason for making honey is so as *I* can eat it." So he began to climb the tree.

He climbed and he climbed and he climbed, and as he climbed he sang a little song to himself. It went like this:

> Isn't it funny
> How a bear likes honey?
> Buzz! Buzz! Buzz!
> I wonder why he does?

Then he climbed a little further . . . and a little further . . . and then just a little further. By time that he had thought of
another song.

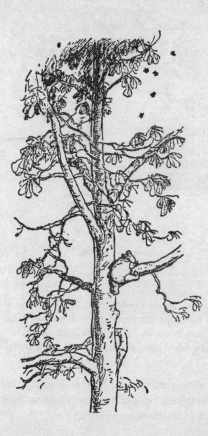

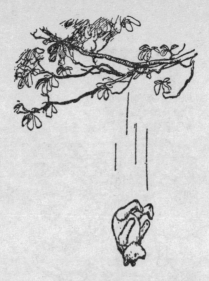

It's a very funny thought that, if Bears were Bees,
They'd build their nests at the *bottom* of trees.
And that being so (if the Bees were Bears),
We shouldn't have to climb up all these stairs.

He was getting rather tired by this time, so that is why he
sang a Complaining Song. He was nearly there now, and if he
just stood on that branch . . .

Crack!

"Oh, help!" said Pooh, as he dropped ten feet on the branch below him.

"If only I hadn't——" he said, as he bounced twenty feet on to the next branch.

"You see, what I *meant* to do," he explained, as he turned head-over-heels, and crashed on to another branch thirty feet below, "what I *meant* to do——"

"Of course, it *was* rather——" he admitted, as he slithered very quickly through the next six branches.

"It all comes, I suppose," he decided, as he said good-bye to the last branch, spun round three times, and flew gracefully into a gorse-bush, "it all comes of *liking* honey so much. Oh, help!"

He crawled out of the gorse-bush, brushed the prickles from his nose, and began to think again. And the first person he thought of was Christopher Robin.

(*"Was that me?" said Christopher Robin in an awed voice, hardly daring to believe it.*

"That was you."

Christopher Robin said nothing, but his eyes got larger and larger, and his face got pinker and pinker.)

So Winnie-the-Pooh went round to his friend Christopher

Robin, who lived behind a green door in another part of the forest.

"Good morning, Christopher Robin," he said.

"Good morning, Winnie-*ther*-Pooh," said you.

"I wonder if you've got such a thing as a balloon about you?"

"A balloon?"

"Yes, I just said to myself coming along: 'I wonder if Christopher Robin has such a thing as a balloon about him?' I just said it to myself, thinking of balloons, and wondering."

"What do you want a balloon for?" you said.

Winnie-the-Pooh looked round to see that nobody was listening, put his paw to his mouth, and said in a deep whisper: *"Honey!"*

"But you don't get honey with balloons!"

"I do," said Pooh.

Well, it just happened that you had been to a party the day before at the house of your friend Piglet, and you had balloons at the party. You had had a big green balloon; and one of Rabbit's relations had had a big blue one, and had left it behind, being really too young to go to a party at all; and so you had brought the green one *and* the blue one home with you.

"Which one would you like?" you asked Pooh.

He put his head between his paws and thought very carefully.

"It's like this," he said. "When you go after honey with a

balloon, the great thing is not to let the bees know you're coming. Now, if you have a green balloon, they might think you were only part of the tree, and not notice you, and if you have a blue balloon, they might think you were only part of the sky, and not notice you, and the question is: Which is most likely?"

"Wouldn't they notice *you* underneath the balloon?" you asked.

"They might or they might not," said Winnie-the-Pooh. "You never can tell with bees." He thought for a moment and said: "I shall try to look like a small black cloud. That will deceive them."

"Then you had better have the blue balloon," you said; and so it was decided.

Well, you both went out with the blue balloon, and you took your gun with you, just in case, as you always did, and Winnie-the-Pooh went to a very muddy place that he knew of, and rolled and rolled until he was black all over; and then, when the balloon was blown up as big as big, and you and Pooh were both holding on to the string, you let go suddenly, and Pooh Bear floated gracefully up into the sky, and stayed there—level with the top of the tree and about twenty feet away from it.

"Hooray!" you shouted.

"Isn't that fine?" shouted Winnie-the-Pooh down to you. "What do I look like?"

"You look like a Bear holding on to a balloon," you said.

"Not," said Pooh anxiously, "—not like a small black cloud in a blue sky?"

"Not very much."

"Ah, well, perhaps from up here it looks different. And, as I say, you never can tell with bees."

There was no wind to blow him nearer to the tree, so there he stayed. He could see the honey, he could smell the honey, but he couldn't quite reach the honey.

After a little while he called down to you.

"Christopher Robin!" he said in a loud whisper.

"Hallo!"

"I think the bees *suspect* something!"

"What sort of thing?"

"I don't know. But something tells me that they're *suspicious!*"

"Perhaps they think that you're after their honey."

"It may be that. You never can tell with bees."

There was another little silence, and then he called down to you again.

"Christopher Robin!"

"Yes?"

"Have you an umbrella in your house?"

"I think so."

"I wish you would bring it out here, and walk up and down with it, and look up at me every now and then, and say 'Tut-tut, it looks like rain.' I think, if you did that, it would help the deception which we are practising on these bees."

Well, you laughed to yourself, "Silly old Bear!" but you didn't say it aloud because you were so fond of him, and you went home for your umbrella.

"Oh, there you are!" called down Winnie-the-Pooh, as soon as you got back to the tree. "I was beginning to get anxious. I have discovered that the bees are now definitely Suspicious."

"Shall I put my umbrella up?" you said.

"Yes, but wait a moment. We must be practical. The im-   13

portant bee to deceive is the Queen Bee. Can you see which
is the Queen Bee from down there?"

"No."

"A pity. Well, now, if you walk up and down with your
umbrella, saying, 'Tut-tut, it looks like rain,' I shall do what
I can by singing a little Cloud Song, such as a cloud might
sing. . . . Go!"

So, while you walked up and down and wondered if it
would rain, Winnie-the-Pooh sang this song:

> How sweet to be a Cloud
>   Floating in the Blue!
> Every little cloud
>   *Always* sings aloud.
>
> "How sweet to be a Cloud
>   Floating in the Blue!"
> It makes him very proud
>   To be a little cloud.

The bees were still buzzing as suspiciously as ever. Some of them, indeed, left their nest and flew all round the cloud as it began the second verse of this song, and one bee sat down on the nose of the cloud for a moment, and then got up again.

"Christopher—*ow!*—Robin," called out the cloud.

"Yes?"

"I have just been thinking, and I have come to a very important decision. *These are the wrong sort of bees.*"

"Are they?"

"Quite the wrong sort. So I should think they would mak
the wrong sort of honey, shouldn't you?"

"Would they?"

"Yes. So I think I shall come down."

"How?" asked you.

Winnie-the-Pooh hadn't thought about this. If he let go
the string, he would fall—*bump*—and he didn't like the ide
of that. So he thought for a long time, and then he said:

"Christopher Robin, you must shoot the balloon with you
gun. Have you got your gun?"

"Of course I have," you said. "But if I do that, it will spo
16 the balloon," you said.

"But if you *don't*," said Pooh, "I shall have to let go, and that would spoil *me*."

When he put it like this, you saw how it was, and you aimed very carefully at the balloon, and fired.

"*Ow!*" said Pooh.

"Did I miss?" you asked.

"You didn't exactly *miss*," said Pooh. "but you missed the balloon."

"I'm so sorry," you said, and you fired again, and this time you hit the balloon, and the air came slowly out, and Winnie-the-Pooh floated down to the ground.

But his arms were so stiff from holding on to the string of the balloon all that time that they stayed up straight in the air for more than a week, and whenever a fly came and settled on his nose he had to blow it off. And I think—but I am not sure—that *that* is why he was always called Pooh.

"Is that the end of the story?" asked Christopher Robin.

"That's the end of that one. There are others."

"About Pooh and Me?"

"And Piglet and Rabbit and all of you. Don't you remember?"

"I do remember, and then when I try to remember, I forget."

"That day when Pooh and Piglet tried to catch the Heffalump——"

"They didn't catch it, did they?"

"No."

"Pooh couldn't, because he hasn't any brain. Did *I* catch it?"

"Well, that comes into the story."

Christopher Robin nodded.

"I do remember," he said, "only Pooh doesn't very well, so that's why he likes having it told to him again. Because then it's a real story and not just a remembering."

"That's just how *I* feel," I said.

Christopher Robin gave a deep sigh, picked his Bear up by the leg, and walked off to the door, trailing Pooh behind him. At the door he turned and said, "Coming to see me have my bath?"

"I might," I said.

"I didn't hurt him when I shot him, did I?"

"Not a bit."

He nodded and went out, and in a moment I heard Winnie-the-Pooh—*bump, bump, bump*—going up the stairs behind him.

BATH MAT

Sneezles

Christopher Robin
Had wheezles
And sneezles,
They bundled him
Into
His bed.
They gave him what goes
With a cold in the nose,
And some more for a cold
In the head.
They wondered
If wheezles
Could turn

Into measles,
If sneezles
Would turn
Into mumps;
They examined his chest
For a rash,
And the rest
Of his body for swellings and lumps.
They sent for some doctors
In sneezles
And wheezles
To tell them what ought
to be done.

All sorts and conditions
Of famous physicians
Came hurrying round
At a run.
They all made a note

Of the state of his throat,
They asked if he suffered from thirst;
They asked if the sneezles
Came *after* the wheezles,
Or if the first sneezle
Came first.
They said, "If you teazle
A sneezle
Or wheezle,
A measle
May easily grow.
But humour or pleazle
The wheezle
Or sneezle,
The measle
Will certainly go."
They expounded the reazles
For sneezles
And wheezles.
The manner of measles
When new.
They said, "If he freezles
In draughts and in breezles,
The PHTHEEZLES
May even ensue."

Christopher Robin
Got up in the morning,
The sneezles had vanished away.

And the look in his eye
Seemed to say to the sky,
"Now, how to amuse them today?"

Us Two

Wherever I am, there's always Pooh,
There's always Pooh and Me.
Whatever I do, he wants to do,
"Where are you going today?" says Pooh:
"Well, that's very odd 'cos I was too.
Let's go together," says Pooh, says he.
"Let's go together," says Pooh.

"What's twice eleven?" I said to Pooh.
("Twice what?" said Pooh to Me.)
"I *think* it ought to be twenty-two."
"Just what I think myself," said Pooh.
"It wasn't an easy sum to do,
But that's what it is," said Pooh, said he.
"That's what it is," said Pooh.

"Let's look for dragons," I said to Pooh.
"Yes, let's," said Pooh to Me.
We crossed the river and found a few—
"Yes, those are dragons all right," said Pooh.
"As soon as I saw their beaks I knew.
That's what they are," said Pooh, said he.
"That's what they are," said Pooh.

"Let's frighten the dragons," I said to Pooh
"That's right," said Pooh to Me.
"*I'm* not afraid," I said to Pooh,
And I held his paw and I shouted "Shoo!
Silly old dragons!"—and off they flew.
"I wasn't afraid," said Pooh, said he,
"I'm *never* afraid with you."

So wherever I am, there's always Pooh,
There's always Pooh and Me.
"What would I do?" I said to Pooh,
"If it wasn't for you," and Pooh said: "True,
It isn't much fun for One, but Two
Can stick together," says Pooh, says he.
"That's how it is," says Pooh.

The Friend

There are lots and lots of people who are always asking
   things,
Like Dates and Pounds-and-ounces and the names of funny
   Kings,
And the answer's either Sixpence or a Hundred Inches Long,
And I know they'll think me silly if I get the answer wrong.

So Pooh and I go whispering, and Pooh looks very bright,
And says, "Well, *I* say sixpence, but I don't suppose
   I'm right."
And then it doesn't matter what the answer ought to be,
Cos if he's right, I'm Right, and if he's wrong, it isn't Me.

Hoppity

Christopher Robin goes
Hoppity, hoppity,

Hoppity, hoppity, hop.
Whenever I tell him
Politely to stop it, he
Says he can't possibly stop.

If he stopped hopping,
   he couldn't go anywhere,
Poor little Christopher
Couldn't go anywhere. . . .
That's why he *always* goes
Hoppity, hoppity,
Hoppity,
Hoppity,
Hop.

Sand-Between-the-Toes

I went down to the shouting sea,
Taking Christopher down with me,
For Nurse had given us sixpence each—
And down we went to the beach.

  We had sand in the eyes and the ears and the nose,
  And sand in the hair, and sand-between-the-toes.
  Whenever a good nor' wester blows,
  Christopher is certain of
  Sand-between-the-toes.

The sea was galloping grey and white;
Christopher clutched his sixpence tight;

We clambered over the humping sand—
And Christopher held my hand.

> We had sand in the eyes and the ears and the nose,
> And sand in the hair, and sand-between-the-toes.
> Whenever a good nor' wester blows,
> Christopher is certain of
> Sand-between-the-toes.

There was a roaring in the sky;
The sea-gulls cried as they blew by;
We tried to talk, but had to shout—
Nobody else was out.

> When we got home, we had sand in the hair,
> In the eyes and the ears and everywhere;
> Whenever a good nor' wester blows,
> Christopher is found with
> Sand-between-the-toes.

Vespers

Little boy kneels at the foot of the bed,
Droops on the little hands little gold head.
Hush! Hush! Whisper who dares!
Christopher Robin is saying his prayers.

God bless Mummy. I know that's right.
Wasn't it fun in the bath tonight?
The cold's so cold, and the hot's so hot.
Oh! *God bless Daddy*—I quite forgot.

If I open my fingers a little bit more,
I can see Nanny's dressing-gown on the door.
It's a beautiful blue, but it hasn't a hood.
Oh! *God bless Nanny and make her good.*

Mine has a hood, and I lie in bed,
And pull the hood right over my head,
And I shut my eyes, and I curl up small,
And nobody knows that I'm there at all.

Oh! *Thank you, God, for a lovely day.*
And what was the other I had to say?
I said "Bless Daddy," so what can it be?
Oh! Now I remember. *God bless Me.*

Little boy kneels at the foot of the bed,
Droops on the little hands little gold head.
Hush! Hush! Whisper who dares!
Christopher Robin is saying his prayers.

Buckingham Palace

They're changing guard at Buckingham Palace—
Christopher Robin went down with Alice.
Alice is marrying one of the guard.
"A soldier's life is terrible hard,"

Says Alice.

They're changing guard at Buckingham Palace—
Christopher Robin went down with Alice.
We saw a guard in a sentry-box.
"One of the sergeants looks after their socks,"

Says Alice.

They're changing guard at Buckingham Palace—
Christopher Robin went down with Alice.
We looked for the King, but he never came.
"Well, God take care of him, all the same,"
                                        Says Alice.

They're changing guard at Buckingham Palace—
Christopher Robin went down with Alice.
They've great big parties inside the grounds.
"I wouldn't be King for a hundred pounds,"
                                        Says Alice.

They're changing guard at Buckingham Palace—
Christopher Robin went down with Alice.
A face looked out, but it wasn't the King's.
"He's much too busy a-signing things,"
                                        Says Alice.

They're changing guard at Buckingham Palace—
Christopher Robin went down with Alice.
"Do you think the King knows all about *me*?"
Sure to, dear, but it's time for tea,"
                                        Says Alice.

Market Square

I had a penny,
A bright new penny,
I took my penny
  To the market square.
I wanted a rabbit,
A little brown rabbit,
And I looked for a rabbit
  'Most everywhere.

For I went to the stall where they sold sweet lavender.
(*"Only a penny for a bunch of lavender!"*)
"Have you got a rabbit, 'cos I don't want lavender?"
  But they hadn't got a rabbit, not anywhere there.

I had a penny,
And I had another penny,
I took my pennies
  To the market square.
I did want a rabbit,
A little baby rabbit,
And I looked for rabbits
  'Most everywhere.

And I went to the stall where they sold fresh mackerel.
("Now then! Tuppence for a fresh-caught mackerel.")
"Have you got a rabbit, 'cos I don't like mackerel?"
 But they hadn't got a rabbit, not anywhere there.

 I found a sixpence,
 A little white sixpence.
 I took it in my hand
  To the market square.
 I was buying my rabbit
 (I do like rabbits),
 And I looked for my rabbit
  'Most everywhere.

So I went to the stall where they sold fine saucepans.
("Walk up, walk up, sixpence for a saucepan!")
"Could I have a rabbit, 'cos we've got two saucepans?"
 But they hadn't got a rabbit, not anywhere there.

 I had nuffin',
 No, I hadn't got nuffin',
 So I didn't go down
  To the market square;
 But I walked on the common,
 The old-gold common . . .
 And I saw little rabbits
  'Most everywhere!

So, I'm sorry for the people who sell fine saucepans,
I'm sorry for the people who sell fresh mackerel,
I'm sorry for the people who sell sweet lavender,
    'Cos they haven't got a rabbit, not anywhere there!

FOR THE BEST IN PAPERBACKS, LOOK FOR THE 🐧

In every corner of the world, on every subject under the sun, Penguin represents quality and variety—the very best in publishing today.

For complete information about books available from Penguin—including Puffins, Penguin Classics, and Arkana—and how to order them, write to us at the appropriate address below. Please note that for copyright reasons the selection of books varies from country to country.

In the United States: Please write to *Consumer Sales, Penguin USA, P.O. Box 999, Dept. 17109, Bergenfield, New Jersey 07621-0120.* VISA and MasterCard holders call 1-800-253-6476 to order all Penguin titles.

In Canada: Please write to *Penguin Books Canada Ltd, 10 Alcorn Avenue, Suite 300, Toronto, Ontario M4V 3B2.*

In the United Kingdom: Please write to *Dept. JC, Penguin Books Ltd, FREEPOST, West Drayton, Middlesex UB7 0BR.*